Mrs. McCready and
The Joy Elf

Mrs. McCready and The Joy Elf

FIRST EDITION

Michael Hume

Yuletime
PUBLISHING COMPANY

COLORADO

Mrs. McCready and The Joy Elf

ISBN 978-1-964046-44-0 (Hardcover)
ISBN 978-1-964046-45-7 (Digital)

Copyright © 2024 by Michael Hume

All rights reserved. No part of this publication may be reproduced, distributed, or transmitted in any form or by any means, including photocopying, recording, or other electronic or mechanical methods without the prior written permission of the publisher. For permission requests, solicit the publisher via the address below.

Yuletime Publishing Company
195 South Rancho Vista Drive
Pueblo West, Colorado 81007
www.firewordsmedia.com

Printed in the United States of America

Original illustrations by Deb McCahan, Johnstown, Colorado (www.debm.art)

Also by Michael Hume:
The 95th Christmas (literary novel)
The Christmas In Me (musical album)
The Innkeeper of Bethlehem (novel – International Best Seller)

Look for ***Mrs. McCready and The Joy Elf*** as part of a new holiday collection, Christmas 2025

For Kathryn:
You are my Heaven

Foreword

Once again, we are blessed by the inspirational experience of Michael Hume, who offers *Mrs. McCready and The Joy Elf* as a heart-warming and soul stimulating adventure into the secret kingdom of ***Life.*** In this story, personal characteristics are ascribed to the "fruits of the Spirit"... you'll meet the "Love Elf," the "Patience Elf," and seven other imaginary characters, including (of course) the Joy Elf himself ... as well as the Joy Elf's new apprentice.

Michael's own personal journey comes to life on these pages, enabling us to glimpse the concealed message of Biblical lore by imagining how true spirituality might "blend" with the imaginary North Pole world that's become part of our modern holiday mythology. Here, the "vacancy of Life" is revealed as our *only* Source for the individual personal traits the self-existent living Spirit desires to share with anyone who embraces the mystery of living from within the confines of that Spirit's prepared container: the soul.

There is a positive blessing in reading this, the latest inspired exposition by a bestselling author who writes to establish the simplicity of the Christian message, pulled from the chronicles of eternity. Your own waning Joy will be revived, revitalized, and replenished when you read *Mrs. McCready and The Joy Elf*, presented here as a prelude to a forthcoming Christmas collection of tales intended to illustrate the qualities of **Life**. Anyone who identifies with pure Spirit, as opposed to creation's temporality, will get something out of the story. Michael draws on his own internal journey to pull us into our own "kingdom of mystery," where God alone is the sole Sovereign of **Life**—of every good feeling, and of all rich, flourishing, divine *fruitfulness*.

–Rev. John S. McCahan

❦

*T*here's one thing you should know about elves.

Elves, if you don't know it, and despite what they say in the movies, are not immortal. Oh, elves live good long lives, to be sure; an elf who eats right, exercises regularly, gets plenty of sleep, and takes the right supplements can expect to live well into his 410s or 420s. Add forty-or-so years for a similarly fit lady elf. But apart from that, and the pointy ears, and their preference for stylish shoes that curl at the toe, an elf's earthly life is not too dissimilar to that of any other person—perhaps not that different from your own. Your average elf starts school as a young child of thirty, enters a trade and marries young (in his sixties), raises a family, grows happily old, and eventually dies and goes home to The Lord.

Probably you don't know these things because you live nowhere near any elfin neighborhoods. That's not a racist thing, or anything like that ... it's just happenstance that elves and people don't live and grow up around each other. For that reason, believe it or not, there are elves in some places in this world who don't even believe in the existence of humans.

But where I come from, we know all about humans, especially the little ones. We really see eye-to-eye with the children—literally! Ha ha! A little elf humor. Ha ha! "Little." Get it?

Which brings me smartly back to the point of my story. And that is, humor and fun and frivolity are all great ways to pass the time, but they're Big Fat Nothin' compared to JOY—real Joy. This I learned, and learned well, one Christmas when The Saint plucked me from my nice cushy job on the toy factory floor and appointed me to a Special Assignment which, frankly, I didn't really deserve.

"Lim'rick," he said, probably because that's the name my papa gave me, "you're gonna learn the difference between joking and Joy. Actually, you're gonna learn all about real, true Joy. You're gonna learn it well! And you're gonna delight all of us by helping a most important person learn it, too.

"Lim'rick, I'm sending you to Heaven."

* * *

Heaven McCready is, in fact, a most important person. She's incredibly blessed. I can't say how many times she too has been plucked, not from cushy jobs but from disaster and even Death itself. From the time, years ago, when her mother chose adoption over abortion; to the fact her new and permanent parents gave her the kind of love you wish every kid could get; to the awesome career and well-deserved professional reputation she enjoyed; to the bountiful gifts of talent, smarts, and good looks with which The Lord saw fit to bestow upon her; you could say Heaven was about the most blessed and aptly named person on the planet. But by the time she became my Assignment, when it came to my department (which is Joy, in case I haven't been clear), Heaven was a hell of a tough cookie.

Once Saint Nicholas—or "Santa Claus," as he's often mispronounced—assigned me to Heaven, my first step was to be inducted as an apprentice member of The Nine. I would only be allowed to join the others full-time if I did a good job with my first Assignment (yes, just like that angel in the movies, but that's a whole different deal with angels, about which I know nothing more than does everybody else who's seen the movie).

It might be helpful if I back up and say a word about The Saint himself. See, most people think he arrived at sainthood due to his generosity with the whole toy thing at Christmas time, and that's certainly a big deal, especially among humans. In fact, I'm pretty sure that's why the *humans* call him "saint." But Nicholas is more than a generous guy who's been sainted by humans—much more. You might say he is a real saint due to what The Lord put in his heart, and therefore in his charge and keeping, and that's where The Nine come in. Each of The Nine elves—assigned to Nick as his personal assistants and barracked in the downtown district of the North Pole neighborhood—is supposed to be a physical representative of one of the nine fruits of the Spirit that you've read so much about.

As you might imagine, that's a hefty responsibility.

There's a Love Elf (Cupid had that job, years ago, before he got promoted, and even though people now think of him only as an arrow-wielding angel, most don't know that he got his start as a plain old elf, just like the rest of us). There's also a Peace Elf, a Patience Elf, and elves for Gentleness, Goodness, Faith, Meekness, and Temperance, of course. Last but not least, there's a Joy Elf, and that Christmas the job was held by an elderly elf by the name of

Frank who was looking to retire, which is where I came into the picture.

"Here's the packet on Heaven McCready," Frank said, an eye blink after I lowered the hand I'd raised to take The Apprentice's Oath. (Come to find out the oaths taken by The Nine and their apprentices are top secret . . . so secret, in fact, that the elves themselves have no idea what they're saying when they take these oaths.)

"This is a pretty thick packet," I said, as I picked up the package Frank had slid across the table in my direction.

"Heaven McCready is a pretty important person," Frank said. "She's blessed. One of the Elect! She's never been out of our sight, since before she was born. So you need to study that packet—thoroughly!—and then I want you on the next sleigh to Denver to do your own observation. I want you to report back to me in forty-eight minutes."

"Forty-eight minutes! It could take me that long to . . ."

"You better get busy," Frank said. "Your sleigh leaves in twelve. Dismissed!"

* * *

One thing you should know about elves is that, compared with humans, we're very fast. Some studies estimate that elves are about one clock notch quicker, on average, than humans. Meaning, to us, a human minute is a second, an hour is a minute, a day is an hour, and so forth.

Some movies do correctly portray elves as being "capable of not being seen" by humans, but they infer that it's because we can somehow make ourselves invisible. Ha! That's a load of coal. The reason we're so hard to see is that we're so dang quick! You think you see something out of the corner of your eye, but you turn to look, and half a second later it's gone. But it's not that the elf is magically invisible, or anything like that. It's just that he was watching you for half a minute from one spot, got bored, and left.

The Saint has that same gift of speed, only it's amplified even more. And his entire fleet of sleighs is, well, VERY fast. Quick as a wink. This, combined with some other forms of elfin assistance which we'll cover later, is how he gets around to *everyone* on The Nice List on Christmas Eve. Nick and his crew can knock out a town the size of Denver in, like, two human minutes, including suburbs.

So when Frank gave me forty-eight minutes to get smart about Heaven McCready, including studying The Packet and conducting my own personal observation, that would've been like giving me two full days, human time. It meant that I would have ample time to develop my own working hypothesis regarding Heaven's Joy Situation, but that Frank didn't want me lollygagging around about it.

From this fact alone, I was able to deduce that Heaven's Joy Situation was generally thought to be fairly dire at that time. And my own analysis confirmed this.

"She's pretty sad," I said, and that was my whole oral report to Frank and the rest of The Nine, roughly forty-five minutes later.

"Depressed?" Frank asked.

"Not that sad."

"Is she considering hurting herself?"

(We always have to rule that out before we proceed with any elfin interventions.)

"I wouldn't say she's suicidal at all," I reported. "More like she's, well, like . . ."

"Empty," offered Faith.

(One thing you should know about elves is that we're not really great at remembering names. In fact,

I couldn't tell you without looking it up what The Faith Elf's name actually is. When we're in conference at The Nine, we just refer to each other by our titles. Those, we never forget.)

"Yes, that's a better description," I said. "I wouldn't think my Assignment is completely empty—not yet—but she's sure more than a couple quarts low at this point."

A little murmur went around the table then, and maybe you could've heard a quiet little gasp or two.

"Oh, my, that's serious," Goodness said. "If Heaven McCready were to run out of Joy completely, well . . . Oh. My. Goodness. Me!"

"The world is already teeming with people who believe they're empty," Peace said. "My department has identified that as the biggest threat we face."

"We simply can't let Heaven McCready—one of the Elect!—go empty," said Love.

"She won't," said Faith. (Faith always says stuff like that. She's very optimistic.) "The Elect are pre-filled, and will always find Joy when they seek it."

"But you still have a job to do," Frank said, looking me in the eye, "and a big job at that."

Everybody waited for my reaction. When it came, it was a little sarcastic, as was my custom at the time.

"So Frank, you've been Joy Elf for, what, three centuries, and now you need a novice like me to try to do what you couldn't do with this one very important person? What's the big deal? I mean, from my perspective? If she can't run empty, what does Heaven McCready need from li'l ol' Lim'rick?"

"Nothing," Frank said. He then gave me that stern look he gives, peering at you with narrow eyes sunk in between the top of his spectacles and the roots of his wildly overgrown eyebrows. "Heaven needs nothing from you. She's one of the Elect, for certain. You, I'm not so sure about. And if you consider your work with her to be a clean-up chore of some kind, you truly are getting started on the wrong pointy foot. Nay, young Master Lim'rick, this job is no chore. Our work is never a burden. This Assignment is a pure golden opportunity.

"As I said, you have a big job to do in Heaven. Because you'll be doing it for your own sake."

* * *

I jumped on the next sleigh headed south. (Actually, they're all headed south.) It's only a nine-second sleigh ride to Denver, but that gave me plenty of time to reminisce about the first time I remember being called out for my youthful inclination toward funny stuff... toward sarcasm... toward humor for humor's sake alone.

I was a mere tad of an elf—a junior high kid of only forty-five or so—and I was apprenticing for what would eventually become my career on the Plush/Stuffed Toy Line. (I did mention that it was a "cushy" job. Ha! Get it?) There were several of us kids working on the line that day, and Yours Truly was cracking everyone up with a steady stream of witty quips. I kept the room filled with laughter!

"Yes, you're keeping the room filled with laughter," said my boss, a crusty old supervisor named Herald. "But I'd rather keep the room filled with Joy."

I was confused.

"Isn't laughing a good thing?" I asked. "Isn't it Joy?"

"Not all the time," Herald said. "In fact, some laughter can be bad. You'll learn the difference someday. That, or you'll end up shoveling coal lumps or cleaning reindeer stalls for a living."

Well, let me tell you, that thought took the sarcastic grin right off my face, and quite quickly.

"Let me ask you a question," Herald said. "And don't answer it right away. You'd probably just have some smart-aleck retort anyway. I want you to think about it."

"Okay," I said, meekly.

"Do you think The Lord blessed you with a sharp mind, and such a quick wit, just to have you constantly wasting your precious gifts on cheap jokes?"

* * *

One thing you should know about elves is that we're extremely good at getting into houses, and doing so without making the slightest sound. No lock can thwart an elf. No alarm system can alert you to an elf's presence on your property. That's why, when chimneys went out of style, The Saint could still get to your decorated tree every Christmas Eve. So getting into Heaven McCready's house on South Grant Street was no trouble at all.

But when I got there to start my assignment on Day One, I found the house empty. I'd just missed Heaven.

"Didn't you know your Assignment wouldn't be home right now?"

I jumped, startled a little, and quickly realized the question had come from Peace. He and Faith were standing right behind me.

"When did you two get here?" I managed.

"Just a second ago," said Faith. "We grabbed the next sleigh, of course. Oh, nobody told you? We always travel in groups. Especially when the Assignment is given to an apprentice . . . but, really, even we seasoned veterans always appreciate the fellowship of our friends when we're on Assignment."

"I see."

"Did you understand my question?" asked Peace. "Maybe you didn't hear me."

"No, I heard you," I said. "But how could I have known my Assignment wouldn't be home right now?"

My new friends exchanged a look. I heard Peace softly remark that they should've brought Patience with them.

"It's okay," Faith said. "We'll go through it together, and I'm sure we'll figure it out. When you did your observation, what did you learn about her pattern, her routine? Where would she be early on a Thursday evening?"

I guess my silence must've been accompanied by a blank stare.

"How carefully did you read your Assignment's diary?" Peace asked.

"She doesn't keep a diary," I quickly responded, feeling pleased that I had at least learned that much about Heaven McCready.

"Well, then, if you didn't read her diary, how did you conclude she was low on Joy?" he asked. "I mean, are you sure you didn't just miss a diary, or a journal of some sort, when you went through everything in the house?"

"I'm positive," I said. "I could tell how little Joy she's finding just by what I read in the packet, and by watching her, and listening in on her phone calls, and looking through her texts and emails, and just seeing how sad she looks all the time. No, if she'd had a diary, I would've found it. I probably would've caught her writing in it. All she has is something called a 'planner,' and all that had in it was . . . wait a minute, yeah, now I remember."

"We'll find her at church."

* * *

One thing you should know about elves is that we prefer brightly colored clothes. We're really fond of yellow and pink . . . bright green and orange . . . reds of just about any shade. So that's why I was taken aback when I saw a bunch of elves in dark and black clothes surrounding Heaven and her colleagues at the church Board of Trustees meeting.

These elves were hard for my friends and I to see, and the humans in the room didn't seem to see them at all. There were several of these dark elves dancing around the conference table, taking turns whispering things in the ears of the people in the meeting.

The meeting seemed to be mostly about a big argument regarding the purchase of new pew cushions for the church sanctuary. Every time a dark elf whispered something in someone's ear, that person seemed to get agitated and either raise their voice, or roll their eyes, or do something else to escalate the fight. "The cushions you want to order are so thin they might as well not be there at all!" one person would say. "That's all we have the budget for!" another would reply. "I just don't care for the color!" another would insist . . . and so on.

The only person who wasn't arguing was Heaven McCready. She just seemed to be taking it all in, though she didn't look happy.

At one point I heard a grey-clad elf whisper something to Heaven about how she should yell at the other people, or something like that. Naturally, I knew yelling at people wouldn't help Heaven's Joy Situation, and I told her so. But she didn't hear me. The grey elf did, though, and he started laughing at me. Soon all the dark elves slowed their wild dance to look in my direction, and before I knew it, they were all pointing and laughing at me in the meanest, most derisive manner possible. While dancing.

(At that moment, I finally understood what ol' Herald had said, years earlier, about some kinds of laughter being bad.)

"Lim'rick!" I heard Peace say. "Let's go! Come outside with us."

So Peace, Faith and I took our leave from the meeting and went outside. It was there that I got my first lesson about daemons.

"They're fallen elves," Peace calmly explained. (Peace always has a calm, soothing manner about him.)

"Oh!" I said. "So that's what fallen elves are. I've heard rumors about them, but I've never seen one before. But why all the snickering? What'd I do that was so funny to those guys?"

Peace and Faith exchanged a quick look.

"You tried to talk to your Assignment," Faith said.

"While she was awake," Peace added.

* * *

Here's what I learned about daemons, also known as fallen elves. Like some people do, occasionally an elf will turn away from The Lord and fall from Grace. In so doing, they forsake all their elvish gifts, all the way down to their very names. They learn to slow themselves down. In fact, they can become about as slow as humans, when they want to. And they can't stay still. Some say it's because they miss the constant speed of their former lives ... but daemons can never stop moving. If they do, they die, and lose all possibility of redemption.

That's why the dark elves I saw in the church boardroom were constantly dancing around. And it's why the people to whom they spoke could hear them—though, as Peace described it, they always whisper so softly in the ears of their Targets that the people think they're only hearing their own thoughts.

"And that's why they laughed at you," Faith said. "They know that elves operate at such a different speed from that of humans that people can't even hear us. Not when they're awake."

I thought about that for a second (which, as humans would reckon it, must be an increment of time which defies measurement).

"Do you mean . . ."

"That's right," Peace said, correctly guessing what I was about to ask, "we can only talk to people when they visit the Other World . . . the world we visit so frequently . . . the world daemons can no longer visit.

"You can only reach your Assignment in her dreams."

* * *

You would think daemons would be allowed to enter dreams . . . and NOT to get into churches.

Faith seemed a little embarrassed when she told me a church was one of a daemon's favorite places to dance around and whisper poisonous things into the ears of the people they chose as their Targets. "After all," Peace added, "many people go to church because they think they'll have actual sanctuary there from evil. You can see the attraction for a daemon: If his Target is ever on guard against the wiles of their daemons, that guard is usually lowered at church."

Hmm, I thought.

"That's why you have to have a lot of, well, ME, I guess, when you interact with people," Goodness said.

I turned around, and sure enough, Goodness and Patience had suddenly arrived on the scene.

"I beg your pardon," I stammered, "a lot of . . . of you? What do you mean by . . .? I mean . . . when did you two get here?"

"We'll take it from here, friends. We'll take it nice and slow, too," said Patience. I realized she was addressing Peace and Faith, who said their quick goodbyes and headed toward the sleigh from which Goodness and Patience must just have emerged.

"Now," Patience continued, "what was your question? Don't rush. We have all the time we need."

I blinked a couple of times, drew breath, and tried to remember what I had asked. "Oh," I finally managed, "what did you mean by—"

"By needing Goodness when you interact with humans?" Goodness interrupted.

"Let him finish, for goodness' sake!" Patience said. "Or, rather, for his sake, I mean to say."

After a brief moment of awkwardness, Goodness issued a sheepish "sorry," and I said yes, that's what I meant.

"Well, you need to show goodness to people, as often as possible, because that's what sets us apart from the daemons."

"I see," I said. And I did.

"I suppose Peace and Faith filled you in on the whole fallen elves matter," Patience said.

"Sure did," I said, "and I just saw a few, right there in church, trying to put the moves on my Assignment."

Goodness clicked his tongue and sighed. "Yep, that's what the evil little buggers do," he said.

"But we're here to help you defeat their efforts, one dream at a time, and however long it takes, you'll help your Assignment find her Joy," Patience said. (I was figuring out that she was *never* in a hurry.)

"One dream at a time?" I said.

"Yes," said Goodness. "I'm sure you know now that the dark ones can't get into her dreams, so that's where you'll be doing your work."

"Okay," I said. But after a quick reflection, I had to ask. "Wait a minute . . . if daemons have lost their ability to dream, why do people have bad dreams? I mean, I've heard that they do, sometimes."

The two elves exchanged a glance. Patience drew a slow breath, then began to explain it to me as only she can.

"There's more to tell you," she said, "and it has to do with the nature of memories. Memories, as such, don't often appear in dreams. That's because memories are created in this world, mostly by people—the created. But dreams are created in the Other World, by the Lord and His helpers. When a memory wanders into a dream, it's because the Lord had a hand in creating it."

"Memories are rarely divine," Goodness added. "Dreams always are."

"Are you with us so far?" Patience asked, giving me time to absorb this revelation. "Yes," I said, "but what does that have to do with bad dreams?"

"What, indeed," Goodness sighed.

"Memories don't often enter *dreams*," Patience said, "but they do create *emotions*. Often, in humans, their memories leave behind very powerful emotions, and not all of those remembered feelings are happy. And though people rarely dream their memories, except perhaps in tiny pieces, the emotions generated by those memories DO get into their dreams, all the time. Even the saddest of emotions."

"Especially when they're low on Joy," Goodness said.

"Right," said Patience. "That's why you're here. As you know, your Assignment's Joy Situation isn't great right now. So I imagine her dreams are kinda sad."

"It's a vicious cycle, really," Goodness said. "Sad dreams deplete access to Joy, which creates more sad dreams, which drain more Joy, et cetera, et cetera. That's why daemons *thrill* at the prospect of making people feel sad. Or angry. Or frightened! They know they can't break into the sacred realm of dreams themselves, but they can plant bad memory feelings like evil seeds in the minds of their Targets, and those seeds can sprout ugly mental weeds that do their dirty work for them."

"Diabolical!" I said.

"Precisely," Patience said. "But—wait for it—there's some good news, too."

"Thank goodness!" I said.

"You're welcome," said Goodness.

"Well, as I'm sure you know, 'time,' as such, means nothing to the Lord. Past, present, future, they're all the same to Him. So occasionally, He'll allow a glimpse into the future to appear in a dream," Patience explained.

"That's why people get that déjà vu feeling," Goodness said. "Like they're experiencing some little thing they've already experienced before."

"Right," said Patience. "So since everything eventually works for *good* for the Lord's Elect, He can show them that He's communicating with them through these déjà vu dreams, and help them see that the future—*their* future—is filled with good gifts."

"Good feelings defeat bad ones, every time," Goodness said, "as long as the person can stand on a foundation of God's gifts. Love. Inner Peace. And, of course, true Joy."

This whole assignment was starting to come into focus for me. It all made sense.

"It all makes sense," I said. "So how do I start? How do I start getting some good feelings into Mrs. McCready's dreams?"

"Good question," Goodness said, "and it's simple, really."

"Just wait until your Assignment falls asleep," Patience said. "Then, just start talking to her. Do your thing. While she's there in the Other World, she'll hear you."

* * *

Goodness and Patience decided to stick around and watch me do my thing for the first time in a Heaven McCready dream. I tried. Really, I did. But I have to say my first trip into her soul was not a stunning success.

For starters, I wasn't there very long. Certainly not long enough to accomplish anything worthwhile. In fact, I later worried that I might've made things worse.

We three elves stuck around in the far corner of Heaven's bedroom, moving every few elf-seconds to avoid detection. Heaven seemed preoccupied, though, and certainly unaware of the fact that she had elves in her bedroom.

She pulled back the covers on her neatly made bed, then sat for a long moment on the side of the bed, seeming to stare at the opposite wall. We had moved behind her by then. After a few moments, I realized she was crying.

I soon felt the urge to go over and try to comfort her, but of course I couldn't do that. She was still awake. But when she looked up at the ceiling and cried, "Why did you leave me all *alone?*" Well, Patience had to practically tackle me to keep me from jumping onto the bed and wrapping Heaven in my best elf-hug. I did blurt out, "You're not alone! I'm here!" —I couldn't help it! Goodness silently clapped his hand over my mouth, and the three of us dove under the bed before Heaven could glimpse us as she looked back over her shoulder.

"A fly?" she whispered, as she grabbed a tissue from her bedside table and wiped her eyes and nose. I poked my own nose over the side of the bed to see her do so, then watched her take another deep breath and climb under her quilt. "How is there a fly in here?" she whispered. "Aren't they out of season by now?"

The three of us got to our feet and waited until Heaven's breathing slowed to a ladylike snore, at which time Goodness nudged me to her bedside to "do my thing."

"I still don't know what I'm supposed to do," I whispered.

"Just close your eyes, breathe, and speak," Patience said. "Keep your eyes closed, and once you start the dialogue, you'll be in. You'll see what she sees in her dream, and you will hear her responses."

"How will I see anything with my eyes closed?" I asked.

"That's just how it works," Goodness offered. "Just like when people dream. When you close your eyes to this world, it becomes possible to see the Other."

"Oh," I said. "I get it." (But I didn't really get it.)

"What do I say?" I asked.

"That's up to you," Patience said.

"Why don't you start with that thing you tried to say before?" Goodness suggested. "You know, the thing about not being alone. We know that's what she fell asleep thinking about."

That sounded like a good idea.

"Sounds like a good idea," I said. "Here goes."

I closed my eyes, and took a deep breath. "Remember to keep your eyes closed until you're ready to leave the dream," I heard Patience say. Then I started:

> *Did you hear me? You're not here alone, you know.*
>
>> Of course I heard you! I know you're here. I'm sorry! I was only gone downstairs for a minute. I didn't hear you. I . . . I . . .
>
> *You didn't hear me?*

In the dream, Heaven spun around, and I saw that she was sobbing. Crying her eyes out, really. She was trying to catch her breath, to compose herself enough to say something. If she did say something, I didn't hear it. I glanced down, saw that I was in a wheelchair, had a sudden realization about that, and quickly decided to open my eyes and get out of Heaven McCready's sad dream. Right away.

* * *

"I told you. I don't know what I'm doing."

"Here, take a sip," Patience said. "Careful. It's hot."

The three of us were sitting at Heaven McCready's kitchen table, which is where we'd skedaddled once I opened my eyes and Heaven had started to stir a bit. Patience had served hot chocolate, somehow instinctively knowing where Heaven kept all the necessary components in her kitchen.

(I don't know how things are in other elfin neighborhoods, but one thing you should know about North Pole elves is that we're experts at making hot chocolate, and we're all discerning connoisseurs of the beverage in all its forms.)

"I think I might've made things worse," I said, after taking a sip from my mug. "I certainly didn't *help* Heaven's Joy Situation. Not at all!"

"Don't worry," Goodness said. "You'll get the hang of it. Everybody has a rough go of it, the first time out."

"Now you tell me!"

"We only heard you say a couple words," Patience said. "Why don't you tell us what you saw and heard in the dream? Take your time. And drink up. No hurry, but don't let it get cold."

Between sips—two sips, if you must know—I told Patience and Goodness all about my brief visit to Heaven's inner world.

"That's it?" Goodness said.

"Don't rush him!" Patience said.

"No, that's it," I said. "As soon as I saw the wheelchair, I realized I was probably in the role of Martin, her late husband, and that the two of them were, at that moment, quite unhappy with each other. I thought I'd better get out of there before I said something I didn't mean. Or that *he* didn't mean. Or that he *did* mean!"

My two companions gave their mugs a quick sip, and gave each other a quick look. "I thought as much," Patience said. "You're definitely gonna need a re-ob. That's okay, though, you have all the time you—"

"What? A re-ob? What's that?"

"A second observation," Goodness said. "Here, take this." He handed me a chunk of plastic. "I swiped it off the charger by her bed as we were skedaddling."

"Is this . . ."

"Her cell phone," he said.

"Okay, hold on," I said. "What do you mean, a 'second observation?' I studied this nice sad lady for forty-eight minutes already."

"Don't be offended," Patience said. "Everybody misses something on their very first observation. Happens to the best of us."

"Now you tell me."

I sat back and looked at the cell phone. I sighed.

"What do I want with this?" I asked. "I already read through her texts. And her emails. Right here on this thing."

"So you know how to unlock it," Goodness confirmed.

"Sure! I watched her put in her code during my *very thorough* observation. Like, four minutes in."

"How many texts did you read?"

"All of them."

"And emails?"

"I went back at least a month. It was almost all work stuff."

After exchanging another look, my two friends both tried to speak at once. "*One* month?" Goodness said, while Patience said "How many emails did she . . ."

I quickly got the idea that they felt my first observation hadn't been as thorough as I'd believed.

"What about social media?" Goodness asked.

"She doesn't use it," I said.

"Never?"

"Not once, for the whole forty-eight minutes."

"Do you supposed she *used* to use social media?"

Well, he had me there.

"You have me there," I said. "I have no idea what she *used* to do."

Goodness and Patience smiled at each other, knowingly, as if they thought they were finally getting through to me.

Patience was the one to break the next clumsy silence. "Very well, Lim'rick, Good job. It sounds like you did as thorough and thoughtful a first observation as any of our apprentices has ever done! Congratulations. You got a fine snapshot of your Assignment's current Joy Situation."

"I agree," said Goodness, and I have to say, the praise was starting to feel good. "Now, it looks like you'll need to go back further. That's what you need a re-ob for."

"Yes," said Patience. "Something has been blocking Heaven McCready from finding the Joy within her, and it seems that blockage didn't occur in the last forty-eight minutes. If it had, you'd have identified it during your excellent first observation."

Goodness and Patience seemed genuine in their encouragement, I thought, but I was starting to feel foolish for not having figured out that I would need more than a current "snapshot" to sufficiently understand my Assignment's Joy Situation.

I broke the next clumsy silence myself. "Okay," I sighed. "I'll try again. Any suggestions?"

They eagerly began to talk over each other again, and Patience finally sat back to let Goodness give his advice first.

"I'd say—just guessing here—you might want to skip back about a year in her email inbox. If you don't see anything interesting there, keep going back in six-month increments. I'm assuming a lady like Heaven has saved a *lot* of emails," he said.

"Great idea," Patience added. "And you'll have to do some sleuthing to see if she had any social media accounts on which she used to be active. People these days reveal a lot about themselves—way too much, really—on those things."

"Also, study every picture you can find," Goodness said.

"I did look at a few of her pictures," I said. "That's why I recognized Martin's wheelchair."

"Great!" said Patience. "Now, go back and look at them all. You might well find something you can use in the next dream."

I was starting to gain a little confidence about carrying out my assignment.

"Will you guys be here tomorrow night?"

"No, our shift is about over," Goodness said. "But a couple of the others will drop by to give you a hand. I'll see if Meekness is available. You wouldn't think it to look at him, but Meekness is a real expert on dream performance. Costumes, makeup, props—you name it, he knows it."

The two elves drained their hot chocolate, and I did the same. We all gave polite belches to signify our pleasure at the treat of each other's company, and Goodness efficiently washed, dried, and replaced the mugs exactly as they'd been found.

"Thanks, friends," I said. "I guess this is goodbye for now."

"I guess so. Are you going to start your re-ob right away?" Patience asked.

"I thought I would."

"That's good," she said. "You should have plenty of time before she wakes up. No need to rush."

"Good luck!" said Goodness. "Oh, and one more thing. If I were you, I'd look for clues about her husband. Find out when he died, and how. Death is notorious for blocking Joy. And, if you can, find out why he was in a wheelchair."

After hugs all around, Patience and Goodness hopped into the next sleigh headed north. (Actually, they were all headed north.) I put in the code to unlock Heaven McCready's phone, and started my "re-ob."

It was an all-nighter. I barely got the phone plugged back in before Heaven woke up. She didn't say anything out loud about it, but I'm sure she was puzzled to find her phone battery down to eleven percent after charging, she assumed, all night.

She probably also wondered why she'd suddenly run so low on milk.

* * *

As I said, it took a good nine minutes—all night—to do my re-ob, and by the time I got Heaven McCready's cell phone back onto its charger and crept out of her bedroom, the first light of day was peeking around the edges of her draperies. I was wiped out ... emotionally exhausted by the things I'd learned, but also just plain pooped. I needed to sleep.

But where?

I didn't want to grab a sleigh for home. I felt like I should stay close to my Assignment while I pondered how I could possibly do anything to help her. I finally got the idea that I could stretch out on a pile of old rugs in Heaven's attic. That attic is used for storage, and I had correctly deduced that, one, there would be room up there, and two, there was zero worry that she might be going up there any time soon. That's because, as I was sitting in her living room overnight, going back over the stuff on her phone, I happened to notice stacks of plastic bins and cardboard boxes, all marked "XMAS," scattered around the living room floor.

One thing you should know about elves, at least the elves in my neighborhood, is that our busy season is always the twelve human months leading up to Christmas. We always know how many human days we have left before we have to have Care Force One (that's The Saint's main sleigh) fully loaded, staffed, and equipped for The Big Night. Stop any North Pole elf on the street and he'll likely be able to tell you the precise current countdown. You know those "X Days 'Til Christmas" novelties you see in your stores, starting (these days) around August every year? Well, in our neighborhood, the countdown to Christmas is no novelty. It's serious. That's why there's a huge electronic ticker-tape type sign, four elves high, on the west wall of the workshop, over by the break room, right above the bulletin board, where you can't miss it. The time clock's over on that same wall, so you can't punch in or out without seeing the countdown. Announcements about shift schedules, meal times, and benefits (The Saint offers a *great* 401[k], by the way) are on that bulletin board, so you can't even find out when the next plum pudding will be without being roundly smitten by the countdown. You might think this would cause stress, but elves don't feel stress the way people do. For us, the countdown just builds excitement and anticipation. Like it does for your kids.

So as you can imagine, I knew beyond the slightest doubt that, at the time I crept up to Heaven McCready's attic, it was December nineteenth. That's because I remembered that when I'd left the day before to start my assignment, it was the eighteenth, since the countdown clock had just started blinking and flashing, which it does when we get within a week of go-time.

When I saw that Heaven (or someone) had taken all the Christmas decorations down from the attic, I knew the coast would be clear for me to get some sleep up there. Also, when I realized, sometime around two-thirty in the morning, that the decorations were still sitting around the living room in bins and boxes on December nineteenth, I had to put down the cell phone for a moment to ponder how this could be possible, and what it might mean. This fact, combined with new information I'd gleaned from a more careful review of things like her "planner," gave me a deeper understanding of just how dire Heaven's Joy Situation actually was.

I was still pondering the things I'd learned overnight when I said my prayers and stretched out on the rug pile in the attic, hoping I could get a full eight minutes' sleep.

But that was not to be.

I'd scarcely closed my eyes when I heard a voice say "You got no shot, joy boy. Widow McCready is mine. *All mine.*"

* * *

He was standing right behind me, stepping from foot to foot the way backup singers do behind their microphone stands at a concert, only about a hundred times as fast. It was the grey elf I'd seen whispering in Heaven's ear at the church meeting.

"Oh, hello," I said. "You're the elf—I mean—the daemon I saw at church."

(Yes, that's really what I said. I couldn't think of anything else. And you'll have to cut me some slack: I'd never spoken to a daemon before, let alone a daemon who'd snuck up on me; and, as I mentioned, I was pretty sleep-deprived at the time.)

"No kidding," he said, only I'm paraphrasing. He didn't use the word "kidding."

His tunic was all grey, in different shades from charcoal to flint, and his skin was the color of the floor of a long-cold fireplace. Thinking back to the church meeting, I realized that all the daemons there had that same grey skin tone—the countenance of corpses. He wore boxy black shoes that looked like bricks of coal, rather than the stylish curled-toe slippers worn by elves. And his eyes looked like dark gold rings around a fiery center of red.

"Well," I said, slowly regaining my composure, "I can't say I'm exactly *pleased* to meet you. But why don't you have a seat, and tell me your name?"

"Nice try," he growled. "I'm sure you know I'm not gonna do either. I just thought, after watching your pitiful performance last night, and seeing you struggle all the way to dawn trying to figure it out on your own, that I'd take pity on you and drop by to let you know you're wasting your time."

"Am I?"

"Most definitely."

"Are you sure it's not *you* who's wasting *your* time?"

"Positive. Look, I understand your optimism, joy boy, misguided though it is. You're new, judging from what I've overheard your new friends saying to you, so you have no idea how wrong they've been, filling you up with all their sunny encouragement. Sure, they've been around the block, but they ain't been around the widow, and they sure weren't around when I dispatched her dear departed hubby."

"Dispatched her ... Martin?"

"Yessiree! Took a while—and Wifey did get in my way, more than once—but I finally drained ol' Marty the Party of anything resembling real Joy, and sent him straight to Hell, laughing all the way. And in the process, I ran the widow down so low she sobs every time she takes a breath. She hasn't smiled in months! She's right on the edge of emptiness herself. So if I were you, I'd hop into the next little toboggan, and get yourself home before you get hurt."

Sleepy as I was, I was starting to put together what he was saying with all I'd learned about Mr. and Mrs. McCready. And it might be self-flattering, but I'll say that something approaching a *plan* was starting to form in my mind.

I decided to ignore most of what the grey daemon said, and to pick out one little fragment that I thought might distract him, or at least give me some confirmation of a couple of things I was starting to consider. "Marty the *Party?*" I said. "Why do you call him that?"

"Oh, yes, he was quite a card. A one-man comedy show! That's why he was my Target. (I'm doing the wife as a bonus, so to speak.) No, I'm a comic myself. I love a good joke. Wanna hear a couple?"

"No."

"Sure you do."

He then rattled off two or three of the most vile, obscene, filthy jokes anyone could imagine. It wasn't hard to keep from encouraging him with laughter: I didn't find his quips the least bit amusing. His telling of them, though, did confirm some things for me. The pieces of my Assignment's puzzle were slowly clicking into place.

As I said, I didn't laugh, but he sure did. He cracked himself up. Finally, when he came up for air, I broke in. "I'm not shocked or surprised by anything you say," I said. "After all, none of it is true. You're a liar, just like your new master, the father of lies."

"You don't know what you're talking about," he said, suddenly serious. "You don't know a thing."

I bluffed: "For one thing, I happen to know for a fact that Mr. McCready didn't go to Hell. You're right, though, when you say he went laughing. He's in Paradise right now, laughing at *you*."

"You ... that's not ..."

"So it *is* you who's wasting time," I said. "You might as well disco off to your next miserable hellish chore. Heaven McCready will find her Joy again, and in the meantime, I'm not the least bit interested in anything a daemon like you has to say."

The grey guy's shuffle slowed then, and I almost thought he might stop altogether. After just a beat, though, he seemed to regain his swagger, and he began stomping all the quicker. Why Heaven McCready didn't come up to investigate the noise was a mystery. Maybe she'd gone outside, or something.

"Ha!" he finally blasted. "Not interested, huh? Well, maybe *this* will capture your interest!"

I didn't know how, but what happened next was that I watched, in my mind's eye, an entire scene between the two McCreadys. It was not a dream.

Intuitively, I understood that the daemon was replaying for me a memory from the mind of my Assignment.

In the scene, Martin McCready was pulled up to the kitchen table in his wheelchair, while Heaven was washing dishes. He did pretty much all the talking, and most of what he said was so wretched and loathsome that I won't repeat it here. He was also wheezing, quite a bit, which didn't surprise me given what I'd read in some of Heaven's older emails.

Between wheezes, he called his wife fat, stupid, selfish, and a few other things you don't need to know about. He delivered each insult with a nasty joke. For example, he resorted more than once to that old junior high standby, the "fat mama" joke, as a vehicle for insulting Heaven about her weight. And he laughed derisively at his own jokes, but when Heaven didn't respond, he would say "Aw, c'mon, babe! Where's your sense of humor? I'm just *kidding* with ya! Tryin' to cheer you up!"

He repeated himself, several times, which also came as no surprise. At least twice, he moaned about how she was just waiting for him to die so she could collect on his life insurance. "I'm sure that's why you leave me sitting all alone for *hours*," he'd say.

Finally, about the third time through the fat mama litany, Heaven had had enough. She threw a plate into the sink, breaking it, and marched out of the room, sobbing uncontrollably.

"C'mon, babe!" Martin called after her. "Where's your sense of humor? I'm *kidding!* Just tryin' to cheer ..."

It was Heaven's memory, and since she was no longer in the room, neither was I. I was back in the attic, with nothing to look at but a grey, grimy, grinning daemon.

* * *

I realized sleep was now out of the question, so I crept downstairs. When I turned to look, I saw no sign of the grey guy ... but I guessed he was still there, hanging around, dancing in the shadows, watching and listening to everything.

When I turned the corner into the living room, I had to jump back. There was my Assignment, stretched out on the very couch where I'd spent the night, lying on her back with a washcloth over her eyes.

"I think she has a headache," said Temperance, in a tone just above a whisper.

"You don't need to whisper, Temp baby," Meekness said. "She's half asleep, and she can't hear us anyway."

"Hi, friends," I said, now becoming accustomed to having colleagues drop in unannounced. "We might still want to watch what we say, though. There's a daemon—"

"I hope it's not too bad," Temperance said. "Come to think of it, I hope it isn't too mild, either."

It was my turn to exchange a look with a fellow elf—this time, with Meekness. "You hope . . . what, now?" I said.

"Her headache," Temperance said, watching the motionless Heaven with what seemed like a fretful gaze. "A really bad headache can completely debilitate you. But a light little nagging headache just bothers you. With the former, you can't do anything. But with the latter, you think you can plug along through your day, but you end up not really getting anything done. With a *medium*-strength headache, you have to take a nap, but you *can* fall asleep. Medium is best, when it comes to headaches," she concluded. "Like with most things!"

"That's *so you*, Temp," Meekness said.

Meekness, who I later learned had served as Artistic Director at the North Pole Little Theatre before being named Meekness Elf, looked the part of Meekness but still spoke in the language of the stage. He was the only one of The Nine who wore glasses, and they were stereotypically taped at the temple and bridge. And he had a tendency to come across more forcefully than he felt—that's what a century or so in the theater business will do to you. But I came to know him as one of the most humble elves I'd ever met. He took bit parts in his own shows, if he took any part at all, in order to model the right attitude for his actors. He always repeated the old saying "there are no small parts, only small actors!" (Actually, at the North Pole Little Theatre, all the actors are small. But that's not the point.) In his note sessions with the cast, he'd always begin by saying, "Just remember, whatever you do, whether you're a star or a stage hand, it's a privilege to be allowed to do it. For every one of you who rehearsed this afternoon, there were twenty or thirty elves at the audition who would've *loved* to sit here and receive the notes I'm about to give . . . but they can't, because we chose *you*."

He once told me his actors groaned whenever he said that.

But I digress.

"I don't know if you heard me," I finally said, "but there's a daemon in the house. He's targeting my Assignment, and he's listening to every word we say."

"No, he isn't, Bubbie," Meekness said.

"Daemons can't hear us any better than people can," Temperance added.

I didn't expect to hear that. In fact, I was pretty sure they were mistaken. "Well, I think this one can," I said. "I just had a very unpleasant conversation with him."

The two turned to look at me.

"Give that line again," Meekness said.

"I said, I just talked to the daemon," I repeated.

"Not too loud!" Temperance said. Then she added, "Not too soft, either."

"Anyway, I'm sure he heard what I was saying."

"Did he start the conversation?" Temperance asked.

"Yes."

"Then it's possible. If he revealed himself to you, it's because he's scared of you, and he wants to try to intimidate you. He must really feel threatened if he came at you so soon," she said.

"And in a situation like that, a daemon can temporarily focus all its energy on listening to you, trying to find something to use against you. But it drains them to speed themselves up like that," Meekness said. "I bet your Assignment isn't the only one napping right now. Ha!"

"Come on, Meek," Temperance said. "You know they can't sleep."

"Can't an elf joke?" he said.

"Well, he also told me he'd overheard my other friends giving me encouragement," I said.

"He lied," Meekness said. "No big surprise there. He was only guessing. Really, a daemon can't hear what we say to each other."

"They're all about talking, not listening," Temperance added. "They have no sense of balance. They're too self-absorbed to really hear what others say. In fact, they don't really want to hear anything *new* at all."

"Yeah, their dialogues are all really monologues," Meekness said. "They already know it all. Ha!"

"What else did it say?" Temperance asked.

"He showed me one of Heaven McCready's memories. A really ugly one, featuring her late husband tearing her down in the most demeaning way."

"That's no surprise, either," Meekness said.

We all watched as Heaven discarded the washcloth and turned onto her side, facing us, but with her eyes closed. She let out a deep sigh.

"Hey," I suddenly said, "daemons are liars, right? So maybe that whole memory was a lie."

"No chance, Babe," Meekness said. "They can't improvise with memories. Whatever you saw was in the original script, if it really was a memory."

"It did seem real enough, based on what I've learned about Heaven's husband," I said.

"I'm so sorry," Temperance said. "I'm sure that must have been a very negative experience for you. But maybe there was something positive in it too?" (Temperance always thinks in terms of balance.)

"I've been thinking about that," I said. "I'm sure it was not the daemon's intent, but that memory might've given me an idea or two that I can use next time she falls asleep."

"Well, that looks like it might happen presto, pal. So, what kind of ideas?" said Meekness.

"For one thing, Martin—that's her late husband—wheezed a lot in that memory. I had learned that he had terrible asthma, and that's why he was wheelchair-bound. The slightest exertion sent him into an attack, so he dare not even try to walk."

"How sad," Temperance said.

"It eventually contributed to his demise," I added. "The daemon caught him during a particularly bad attack and panicked him. It squeezed the breath right out of him."

"That's horrible!" Meekness said. "How did you find that out?"

"I pieced it together from Heaven's old emails that he'd died that way, but the little 'memory show' really brought it home to me," I said. "But that's not all. According to those emails, Martin also had what they call 'early onset dementia,' and in the memory, he did repeat things, like he'd already forgotten that he'd said them before. So the whole scene drove that home for me, too."

"Early onset dementia!" Temperance said. "Dreadful!"

"Yep," I said. "But I think the onset of *daemon* is what really got him. In the end, he probably just lost the will to keep fighting."

"Such a tragedy," Meekness said.

"True," I said, "but here's something that will appeal to both of you. As you know, Tragedy in the theater is balanced by Comedy. And comedy might just hold one of the keys to helping Heaven find her way back to Joy."

"Boffo!" said Meekness.

"How do you mean?" said Temperance.

"Snaa-aa-aahxhx," said Heaven McCready.

(She'd started to snore.)

"Come with me," I said. "I'll show you. I'm gonna try something."

"Outstanding!" Meekness said. "The young apprentice here is all, *'hold my hot chocolate!'* Ha!"

Neither Temperance nor I knew what that meant, but we let it go, and we all crept up to the couch, where Heaven McCready was starting to dream.

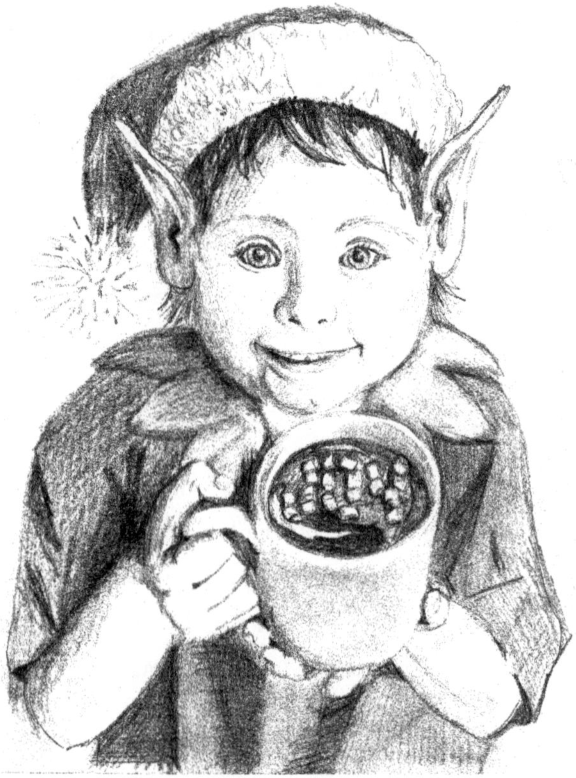

*   *   *

G'night, Murphochs! See ya next year!

Merry Christmas!

The scene was the conclusion of the McCreadys' "Christmas Eve Eve" party, some several years ago. It wasn't a memory, per se. I was just putting Heaven in a familiar setting from happier times (I guessed), when she and Martin hosted a small dinner party each December twenty-third. I'd learned this from the research I'd done on some very old emails, and I knew to look for emails in mid-December from years gone by, because I'd seen this notation on December twenty-third of this year in her planner:

~~XMAS EVE EVE~~
no point

I'd also learned that Ed Murphy and his wife, Cookie Murdoch, never missed a McCready Christmas Eve Eve party, before Ed passed away, and that the McCreadys' pet name for the couple was a mixture of their last names. I guessed that "G'night, Murphochs" would be the right line to put us in the scene, and as it turns out, I was right.

That joke never gets old.

What joke?

"See ya next year."

Oh, brother. That joke's been old a long time.

Well, we won't see them again until after the first, so . . .

Shut up, funny boy. Kiss me.

I did. We were standing under the mistletoe Heaven always hung in their front hall (per old photos), so I kinda had to lay a smooch on her. Or, rather, Martin did.

Hey, they're playing our song.

Who they?

I believe it's Glen Dorsey. Or Perry Miller Tommy Como . . . I don't know. Whoever's on that old Christmas CD.

Oh, yeah, it's still running. I'll shut it off.

Dance with me first!

It was *The Christmas Waltz*, which I conjured into the dream by clumsily humming a few bars. And it probably wasn't any of the famous bands I'd joked about.

We waltzed.

This is our song? The Christmas Waltz?

> Is that what this is? I thought it was Fogelberg.

Wow, you're really full of it tonight. You know how I feel about funny boys, though.

She always said she didn't like them. It was a running inside joke between the two of them. I can't recall where I found that little gem ... maybe from some old voicemails from Martin, from before asthma and dementia changed him into the jerk I'd seen in the daemon's memory show. She'd never deleted any of those messages, which preserved his "old" voice to remind her (and to inform me) of who Martin really was.

Well, you married one.

> Just one. So far.

> *Oh! Now who's got jokes? Hey, here's something a little more upbeat! Giddy-up, giddy-up, giddy-up, let's go!*

I conjured *Sleigh Ride* by the Boston Pops. That one, everybody knows.

I remember thinking this was really working. In this dream, up to that point, Heaven seemed genuinely happy. Would dreams like this help her find her Joy? I hoped so. I didn't know what else to try.

I kicked my giddy-upping into top gear, prancing high-knee style around the living room, and she actually started laughing. It was good, happy laughter, too!

Then came the wheezing.

> Just sit down, Mart! I'll get your inhaler.

> *I'm (wheeze) okay. . . It's just (wheeze) a mild one. It'll (wheeze) pass.*

> I can't find it! Where is it?

The scene changed abruptly, like they do in dreams, and suddenly we were in a hospital room. I was in the bed, and Heaven was frantically searching through her purse, presumably for Martin's inhaler.

> I can't find it! I can't find it! Oh God!

I couldn't think of anything to say. And I didn't want her tormented dream to set me wheezing again.

> Oh God! Doctor! Nurse! I can't find it! He's dying! He's dying! Oh God, I killed him.

I was certain this wasn't a memory. I'd learned that Martin had died at home. Heaven found him when she got home from work. But I also understood that this happy dream had been transformed to a nightmare by her heretofore unshakable guilt over not being home when Martin died.

> Oh God. I killed him.

Needless to say, it was time to bail out.

> I can't find it . . .

* * *

As if that dream hadn't ended badly enough, what happened next was worse. And it could've resulted in a real disaster.

I opened my eyes, and a people-second later, Heaven opened hers!

She sat up, and she stared at me. We both froze! Then, she reached up and rubbed both eyes. I finally snapped out of it and bolted around behind the couch, where Meekness and Temperance had been frantically motioning to me. We ducked out of sight when my Assignment stood up and began looking around.

"Whoa," was all she said aloud. We then peeked out to see her slowly walk off in the direction of her guest bathroom.

"Did she see you?" Temperance asked.

"Oh, yeah," I said.

"Maybe she only got half a glimpse?"

"No, she got a good full look at me," I said. "I'm sure of it."

Meekness broke a brief silence then, with "Well, that's a big no-no, Buddy, as I'm sure you know. This can happen when you don't skedaddle right away after you bail out of a dream. It can wreck the assignment if they start to think they're going nuts, because they might stop paying attention to their dreams. Or stop dreaming altogether. Ouch!"

"Now you tell me."

"Oh, well, now you know," he said.

"I'm sure you're still all right," Temperance said. "She seemed to react as though seeing you was just a continuation of the dream—like she hadn't really been awake yet."

"I guess I'll find out eventually," I said.

"Why'd you freeze?" Meekness asked.

I sighed. "I don't know. All I know is that I'm knackered. I haven't slept in about thirty-six minutes."

"Ouch!" he said. "Let's get you somewhere where you can catch a few z's! But first: how was the dream? Take it from the top."

I recounted the dream as the three of us strolled out of sight to the kitchen. Temperance got some cocoa out of the pantry, but I shook my head, knowing Heaven could walk in at any moment.

"Sounds like you were starting to make progress," she said, as she replaced the cocoa exactly as she'd found it. "It's good to know she can still bring up some positive emotions. A few more dreams like that, and maybe . . ."

"Yeah, you're right, Temp baby," Meekness said. "Sounds like she still has some bad feelings to work through too, though."

"Well, she's lost the love of her life, and that means her feelings will always be mixed, whenever she thinks of him," Temperance responded. "So far, the scales have been tipped in the unfortunate favor of her sadness, and maybe anger over the way he became at the end of his life. The way he treated her. In her rational mind, she knows he didn't really mean to hurt her. He loved her! But her heart is clearly struggling with moving beyond those bad memories and getting the scales to tip back in favor of happiness."

"That's why you're here, kiddo!" Meekness said, addressing me.

"Of course," I said.

"Like Temp said, though, you're probably gonna need a few more happy dreams. But happiness is fleeting," Meekness said. "Comes and goes, based on the stuff that happens. Joy is different: it's a gift from The Big Boss. When you help this lady get back to her Joy, she'll have what she really needs, no matter what ups and downs she runs into before her curtain call."

"And then the scales will tip back," Temperance said, a big smile lighting her face. "And stay that way!"

"I hope you're right," I said. I let out a yawn I couldn't suppress. "I was just hoping to help Heaven before Christmas, and I'm running out of time."

"Time," Temperance repeated. "I understand. But you'll see. It will happen, and it'll happen exactly when it's supposed to happen. No earlier, and no later."

"Well," Meekness said, "that's the end of our scene. Seems like it's time for your exit, too. You need an intermission, my friend!"

"I thought I should stay close," I said, "at least until..."

"Why don't you ride back with us, get a short—no, long—no, *medium* nap, and come back a little closer to bedtime?" Temperance suggested.

I yawned again.

"Okay," I said. "I might do better after a snooze. I could hardly do worse."

"I'll call us a sleigh," Meekness said.

"Thanks," I said. "By the way... I know it's the *worst* time of year to ask, but do you think it'd be possible to get a quick meeting with The Saint? I mean, after my nap? I could sure use some mid-assignment fatherly advice."

"Check with Frank first," Temperance suggested.

"Yeah, babe," said Meekness. "He might want the first crack at it. After all, technically, Frank's still The Joy Elf. He knows his stuff, too. But if he can't help you, I'm sure he can hook you up with The Saint."

"Good," I managed. "Good idea."

I didn't mention it to my two helpful colleagues, but I was thinking at that point that I might offer to resign. At least, I wanted to see if Nick was having any second thoughts about his choice for Joy Elf Apprentice.

* * *

One thing you should know about elves is that we don't tend to use newfangled technology much. We know how it works—we're not stupid, and after all, we *make* a lot of those gadgets you humans always ask for in your letters to "Santa." And you'll recall that I had no trouble navigating Heaven's "smart phone" and laptop. But we don't use those things ourselves. About the only "screen" we really use is the giant countdown clock in the workshop. But I already mentioned that. I'm just saying this by way of explaining that we don't call for our ride-shares the way you call for yours. We literally just *call*.

So we stepped outside, and Meekness lifted his head to the sky and hollered "Yo! Sleigh! Three headed north!"

Nothing happened right away, so he repeated the call a couple of human minutes later, and before he could get to the word "north," a sleigh landed in Heaven McCready's yard.

(People never see this kind of thing happening. Remember, it happens so quickly, it's practically invisible.)

"What's the holdup?" Meekness asked the driver, a young elf who introduced himself as Lyric, once we topped the thick December clouds over Cheyenne.

Lyric gestured by jerking his head over his shoulder, and said, "Had to pick her up. Insisted she come down and ride back with you. Plus, have you seen the countdown lately, Mac? Everyone's a little busy right now."

Meekness agreed. "Right. Sorry, kiddo," he said. He and Lyric continued chatting for the rest of the ride.

"Do you remember me?" said our fellow passenger, a lovely older elf who looked like anyone's kindly grandma.

"Gentleness, aren't you?" I guessed.

"That's right," she said. "Come here."

Gentleness said no more words, but simply folded me in her arms in the warmest, most tender embrace I'd ever enjoyed. It was a true delight, and a most welcome blessing.

She softly caressed my neck, and it reminded me of the way my mama would hold and comfort me when, as a little elf, I would become frightened, or sick. Relief washed over me in waves, and I'm sure we hadn't even made it to Helena before I fell fast asleep.

Almost immediately, I began to dream.

* * *

At first, I didn't know I was dreaming. I found myself sitting with The Saint in the executive conference room, and I assumed Meekness and Temperance had gone ahead and arranged for my coaching session. I should've realized something was different, though. Nick was certainly different. It looked like the Saint Nicholas I knew, except it looked like a Santa made entirely of light. Really, I couldn't even look directly at him.

"Do you know who I am?" he said.

"Aren't you the boss? Mister—Saint—Nicholas? Sir?"

He laughed. It was a genuine, hearty, jolly laugh.

(By the way, I should clear up something about "Santa," because you humans have a common misperception about him. Way back when, somebody cracked a joke in the break room, and Nick gave a HO-HO-HO laugh. Okay, he *did* laugh that way, and he still does, sometimes. But this became an example of how people tend to stereotype others, right down to the way they laugh. It might surprise you to know that Nick sometimes uses a Ha Ha laugh. Other times, he'll let loose with a Hee Hee. He snickers. He giggles. He'll even blast out a single HA! on occasion. But *one time,* he HO-HO-HOs, and ever since, the whole world thinks that's the only way he knows how to laugh. A load of coal, if you ask me.)

"I'm sure I look like him to your eyes," he said, "but no, Lim'rick. As Nicholas gives an elf like you an assignment, I AM the One who gives assignments to him, and to everyone else I choose."

I knew then that I was dreaming, but I dropped down right onto my face anyway. You always hear about folks doing that in situations like this, and you might think they do it by choice . . . but I can assure you, it isn't optional. It just happens.

He continued. "A long time ago, as you would reckon it, I gave an assignment to a guy named Elihu, and though I'm sure you read all about it in school—unless you faked that book report—let Me remind you of what I had him say to *his* Assignment: a guy named Job."

Now, from that point, all the way to the end of the dream, all I could recall "hearing" was a thing which I'm gonna have trouble describing. It was a Voice, I guess, but it wasn't like any voice I'd ever heard before, nor could possibly have imagined. Have you ever heard a huge flock of birds landing together in a field, or on a little lake? Well, it sounded like that, kinda, except it would've been the sound of the wings of about a thousand such flocks. And that's not all. You know the sound a big roaring campfire makes? Imagine about a million big campfires, all roaring together, along with the massive wing sound. And as if that weren't mighty enough ... do you know the sound of a "Class Five" rapid on a river—the kind of rapid even expert kayakers have trouble navigating? Imagine a Class Five Bazillion rapid, rushing loudly along, joined by ten thousand mile-high waterfalls. Plus the wings, plus the flames. Plus, you can toss in about a thousand loud choirs, all singing "Ah," with unearthly breath control. That wouldn't really describe this Voice in full. But it's as close as I can get you.

As I mentioned, I was *kinda* hearing this indescribable Voice, but—and this might seem unusual to you—more than hearing It, I *felt It*. I felt It filling me up, so to speak. This Voice filled me up with a few different *understandings,* I guess, all at once; and I can only try in a poor and inadequate way to explain what I woke up simply knowing:

> *First, you need to re-read what Elihu said about dreams to Job. I know you faked that book report, so I'll give you a clue—I put it in Chapter 33.*
>
> *Second, you can't give Joy to Heaven McCready. I AM the only One who can do that, and I've already given her all she needs. I'm doing both of you a big favor—we call this a "blessing"—by letting you help her find again the Joy within her. The Joy she's always had. Her once and future gem.*
>
> *I've held that girl in the palm of My hand since before she was born. No way I'll abandon her to the poison of her daemons.*

And by the way, you were right when you guessed her husband hadn't gone into the eternal pit, but you guessed wrong about the daemon, or asthma, squeezing him to death. I AM the only One who can withdraw the Breath of Life, and I did so to rescue that funny boy from his agony. He and I are still laughing about it. He finally gets it.

Lastly, an assignment like this one usually takes more time, but for the sake of both you and my daughter Heaven—and because time means nothing to Me—I'm going to let you wrap it up right away. You both have everything you need. Don't try to plan it out. When the "time" comes, I'll put the words right in your mouth, so to speak.

Get it?

* * *

I was jolted out of the dream by the voice of Lyric.

"C'mon, Sleepy. Wake up. End of the line. I gotta be in Miami in twelve seconds. Get it?"

"Five more seconds," I murmured.

I felt Gentleness release her hold from me, then heard her say gently (how else?): "Time to go, Lim'rick. There's someone here you'll want to get to know."

I opened my eyes, and right there on the platform was a beautiful—or handsome?—bright, shining elf, extending a hand to help me out of the sleigh. I took the hand—it was very warm—and I climbed out. I then helped Gentleness out, and she said a soft goodbye and slowly walked into the Sleigh Depot. Lyric briskly whipped the reins, and his sleigh took off like a shot. The shiny elf and I had the platform to ourselves.

"Do you remember me?" said Shiny. "We've met, but it was many minutes ago."

"Love?" I said.

"At your service. The Saint asked me to meet you, and to talk with you about a few things before you head back to your Assignment."

After that dream, I was no longer thinking about resigning. I was only looking forward to the next dream I'd be able to share with Heaven McCready.

"That's great," I said. "I was hoping you'd be available to help with my Assignment's next dream. Will you ride back with me?"

"No," Love said, "but I'll definitely be helping you."

"From here?" I said. "Like, a live remote, or something?"

After a sweet laugh, Love replied: "Lim'rick, you're such a joy. Literally now, I guess!"

Now look who's got jokes, I thought.

"I'm sure you know—unless you faked that book report—that *Love is with you always.*

I hadn't faked that one.

"Right," I said. "I remember. I should've known."

"Will you walk a bit with me?"

It came as a welcome surprise when Love took my hand and led me down a snowy, pine-flanked trail into the forest.

(One thing you should know about elves is that we never get too hot, or too cold, and this is true even though we dress the same in all seasons. Some say it's because of the amazing fabric from which our clothes are made. It really is incredible, and unbelievably comfortable. One size truly does fit all elves, too. Come to think of it, elves only come in one size.

Anyway, I don't know why humans don't have this stuff. I guess it's because nobody on the Nice List has ever thought to ask for "amazing clothes that keep you warm *and* cool, all the time, that always fit, and never need ironing" in their letters to Santa. You'd think it was some kind of magic, but it's really just this nifty fabric. So maybe that's why elves can walk around in the brisk environs of the North Pole, where it *does* get a little chilly, without so much as a slight shiver. Or maybe it's just a function of elf biology.)

"Speaking of biology," I blurted, "I have to ask. Not that it matters, and maybe it isn't even any of my business: but are you a lady elf, or a guy? I honestly can't tell."

Love laughed again, and there was no meanness in it.

"Pardon my bluntness," I said. I probably blushed. Elves blush sometimes.

"I'm both, of course," Love said. "I know you didn't fake *that* book report. Who would? But you'll recall that one of the main traits we share with humans is that we're made in God's image. *'Male AND Female created He them.'* So I'm both, and so are you."

I spent a few speechless elf-seconds pondering this.

"But since you brought up the subject of biology, yes, the Lord gives our physical bodies one gender or the other, because He wants us to learn of Him from a particular perspective," Love said.

"So . . . are you . . . I'm so sorry."

"I'm a lady," she said. "My mama named me Shiny, but you can call me Love."

(I guessed right on the name! What're the odds?)

"And since you're sure to ask, I'll tell you about the light," she said. "My name is Shiny, but I don't really shine of my own accord. What you see is God's light—the Light of Heaven—reflecting from me. But it's just a preview. When you meet that special someone with whom you'll want to share your journey, you'll see this Light again, endlessly reflecting from her."

* * *

I'll always be grateful for that opportunity to walk and talk with Love before heading off to complete my assignment with Heaven McCready. It was an incredible experience for me. I asked her what it was like to have the responsibility of representing the very nature of the Lord Himself, and said that I guessed it must be a hefty duty. She told me it wasn't too hefty at all. "His yoke really is easy," she said, with a warm laugh, "and His burden really is Light!"

She pointed out the difference between God, who's a hundred percent Love and Light, and herself—a mere elfin representative of Love, with a polished complexion off of which light seems to enjoy bouncing.

"So," Love said, as we found a nice bench, "do you think you're starting to learn the true nature of Joy?"

"Starting," I said. "I know my Assignment, Heaven McCready, prayed for it. Kinda. What I heard her ask for when I was hanging around during my first observation was to stop being sad all the time. And I had already been assigned to her, so she was—".

"She was on her way to rediscovering her Joy, even before she asked," Love said. "That's SO God."

"It so is!"

"And you know by now, I'm sure, that your assignment was not to *give* her Joy. She already had all she needed, and always will have."

"I figured that out," I said.

"All you can do is to try to help her find it again, behind all the antics of her daemons. Oh, they'll keep trying to drag her down, but if you can help amplify the Voice of Joy within her, it will absolutely overwhelm and drown out the demonic voices trying to distract her."

I sat back, and blew out some air.

"I see that now," I said. "Are you sure you don't want to tag along, just for fun? I wouldn't refuse the support."

"No," she said, "you'll be fine. You have what you need now. What Heaven McCready needs is Joy, and that's your department."

"True," I said. "I can tell she hasn't been having any trouble finding her other gifts. Love is never far from her. In fact, it's her deep love for her late husband that's giving her daemon a chance to make her feel sad all the time. She misses Mr. McCready. She misses the guy he once was, before he got sick, an awful lot."

The two of us sat in silence for a bit, and watched as a festive light snow began to decorate the forest.

"There's a reason you were chosen for this assignment, Lim'rick. Behind all the jokes and sarcasm, you've really been a joyful elf, all your life. Joy has lived in you, and has protected your soul, even in times of sorrow. That's what your Assignment needs now. Joy will bring her through her sorrow, too. You'll see."

I thought about that, all the way through my ride back to South Grant Street in Denver. (The holiday sleigh traffic was pretty backed up . . . it took almost fifteen seconds to get there.)

When I got inside, Heaven was downstairs—I could hear the sound of her television. That gave me a chance to take one more look at the planner she always left on the end of her kitchen counter. I'd seen all her emails and texts, listened to all her voicemails, and learned that she had never used social media. But there was one thing in the back of that planner that I'd been meaning to check out, and I wanted to give it a look before bedtime.

* * *

It's right behind those trees.

I don't see it.

I know I'm relatively young, as adult elves go. And I'd be the youngest member of The Nine, if this dream worked out the way I believed it would. But I *am* a grown-up. I'm almost eighty. (Because I'm single, and admittedly somewhat "playful," folks think I'm even younger.) I've been working in the toy shop for decades, so I know something about the way things used to be. That's why I knew what I was looking at when I'd found the little envelope tucked in the back inside flap of Heaven's planner. It contained something called "photographs," which is what pictures were back in the day. We used to get lots of requests for a thing called a "camera" in letters to Santa. This was a device people used to use to collect pictures. Now, they easily take pictures of everything, because they all carry around devices which are part computer and part camera (oh, and part telephone), and that's much easier than taking pictures with those ancient camera-only cameras, since back then, you had to remove a thing called "film" from the camera and take it to the drug store and then wait two-to-seven days before you could go back and collect your pictures, which were printed on a special type of paper and stuffed into little envelopes like the one

I found in Heaven's planner. So I knew that they were pictures, and I knew they had to be at least a quarter-century old.

From my careful analysis of these "photos," I learned that, years ago, Martin and Heaven had gone hiking one day in the mountains, and Heaven had "photographed" the event. One of the pictures showed a young Martin, standing in front of a thick stand of trees; on the back of this picture, someone (probably Heaven, based on my initial handwriting analysis) had written "Marty and his invisible waterfall." He looked like he was in his twenties, so I deduced that these photos—and the hike they documented—had been taken pretty early in the McCreadys' romantic relationship. They might even be pre-marital photos, I further deduced. So I tried to start the dream by putting Heaven back in that scene. Something told me it had been a happy day, and that it might even have created a good memory in which the Lord might have had a hand.

> *It's right over there, behind those trees.*
>
> > Where? Where do you see a waterfall?

I don't.

Then how do you know there is one?

I can hear it. I know what waterfalls sound like.

Then, as He'd promised, The Lord put a new set of words into my mouth. I know, because I wouldn't have thought them up myself.

Just like sheep.

Sheep? Are you being funny again?

Not at all. Sheep know their Shepherd's voice, right? And I know what waterfalls sound like.

Oh.

Right?

No joke?

No joke.

I wanna see this waterfall.

Okay, let's go. Careful, though. Might be steep.

I can't see it.

Just through here . . .

I can't find it! Oh God!

I knew this might happen. Heaven's old feelings of guilt and fear turned the happy hiking scene back into the dreadful hospital room.

Oh God! He's dying! I'm killing . . .

I was ready for it this time, though. That's because, after I found the photos in Heaven's planner, I decided to go back and look in her bedroom, while she was still watching television downstairs, to see if there were any old scrapbooks or photos I might've missed during my observation. I didn't find any pictures, but I did find a very old trophy tucked away on a high shelf in her closet. Engraved on the trophy was the title *"Third Grade Softball – CHAMPIONS,"* along with the names of the champion players. One of those names was "Heaven Thompson." Another was "Martin McCready."

I heard Heaven switch off the television, and I guess I panicked. I dropped the trophy onto the closet floor, right under the spot where her bathrobe was hanging. No time to scramble up and put it back where I'd found it—I could hear her coming up the stairs. So I skedaddled under the bed, and waited for the sound of her ladylike snoring. When it came, I started the dream, but I had this third-grade softball image in my mind, and it came in handy later, in the scary hospital scene.

Instinctively, I knew just what to do.

From the hospital bed, without making a sound, and therefore without wheezing . . . I started making funny faces at Heaven.

>What are you doing?

Ooh ooh ee ee ee!

I scratched under my arms, completing the monkey look.

>You're weird.

Ooh ooh ooh!

I pretended to pick a bug out of young Heaven's hair, and—what else?—to eat the bug.

Ooh ooh ah ah ah!!

>Stop it!

Ooh ooh ooh!

HONEY, DON'T YOU LIKE
MARTY? DON'T YOU THINK
HE'S FUNNY?

I'm not sure who said that, but it came from the bleachers behind where we kids were sitting on the dugout bench. I guessed it was Heaven's mama.

No.

Ooh ooh ee ee ee!

I don't like funny boys.

You married one.

So you keep reminding me.

Suddenly, the McCreadys were an old married couple. We were in the car. Heaven was driving, and she looked the way she had the day I did my first observation, so I guessed we were in a recent scene. But when I looked down, "Martin" was younger. And when I spoke, he didn't wheeze.

Departures. There you go.

We were arriving at an airport. But it wasn't the Denver airport, and I guessed it wasn't any other airport Heaven had ever seen, either. It was being created for us, right then and there, and suddenly, I understood what it meant.

Do you know which gate?

I think there's only one.

Oh, right.

Thanks for a great ride! Ride of my life! Never in all my days have I had such a tremendous ride, all the way to the airport!

Funny boy. Right to the end.

Heaven parked, and we got out of the car. We could hear the usual airport sounds: take-offs, landings, unintelligible loudspeaker announcements.

Luggage?

It's all been checked.

We kissed, like married couples do before one of them boards a plane, or a train, or an ocean liner, or whatever they imagine will take them to their Destination.

Got anything to say?

I smiled.

Look, I told you I loved you already.

When? When did you say that?

The day we got married. As I said then, if things change, I'll let you know.

Funny boy. Still just can't say the words, can you.

At this point I seemed to step onto one of those moving sidewalks, like the ones you see in airports. I was looking back at Heaven, who was getting smaller and smaller. I somehow knew she was starting to tear up, though pretty soon, I was too far away to see details like that.

Something inside me told me it was time to do what I'd been assigned to do. I ran back to Heaven and folded her in a tight embrace. And when we pulled apart to look into each other's eyes, we could feel the crisp mountain air, and we could hear the waterfall.

It's time. I have to go.

I know.

Now she was crying, full-on, tears flowing down her cheeks as if to mimic the unseen cascade. I reached up and wiped her tears away.

But let's find that waterfall first. Together. Will you help me look?

Heaven laughed through her tears.

> Are you kidding?

No.

A sniffle.

> Okay, lead on.

I took her hand and slowly we began walking toward the stand of trees. The waterfall rushed more loudly. We could also hear the soft strains of Dan Fogelberg's guitar, and just a hint of his vocal on *Longer*.

I love you, Heaven. I always have, and I always will. You're the most beautiful, wonderful thing I've ever imagined, let alone seen. You truly are Heaven! And I don't want to leave you. I love you. I love you! And that, my love, is no joke.

The tears flowed like a river now, but I realized they were no longer tears of sadness. Dare I say it? At that moment, I had the very clear impression that Heaven McCready had found such a deep reservoir of Joy inside her that she couldn't keep it in ... couldn't keep it from pouring out and running down her face like an overflowing wellspring.

Like a waterfall.

We walked through the mountain forest, hand in hand, for an eternity. And that's where I left Mr. and Mrs. McCready when I opened my eyes, took just an elf-second to watch her smile-crying in her sleep, and then skedaddled to the kitchen to see about a cup of hot chocolate.

* * *

I wasn't a bit surprised to find Gentleness waiting for me at the kitchen table. She added marshmallows to the steaming mug of chocolate she'd just poured for me, and I pulled up a chair to join her.

She didn't say much. She never does. I later learned, though, that when she does say something, it's generally filled with tender wisdom. We just enjoyed our hot chocolate, and once we'd finished our mugs and belched (I'd never heard such a gentle burp!), I washed up, and she put everything back where she'd found it.

"Nothing to do now but wait," she softly remarked.

"I guess you're right," I said. "But—and I know I'm new here—may I ask what we're waiting for?"

"Confirmation."

I thought I understood. So we just sat together in silence as the dawn began to show itself, and then we skedaddled out of sight to the formal dining room when we heard Heaven McCready's footsteps on the back hallway floor.

The daemon was there in the dining room, dancing around in a dark corner. I made brief eye contact with him—long enough to see the terrified look on his face—before he skedaddled off to some other part of the house.

Gentleness and I peeked around the corner to see Heaven shuffle into her kitchen, open her planner, and take her cell phone out of the pocket of her robe. She also placed her third-grade softball trophy on the counter nearby.

Heaven punched the screen a couple of times with her index finger, then put the phone to her ear.

"Cookie? Hi. Hi, Hi! Yes, thanks. Better. Yeah, a little better. I had an amazing dr—I had an amazing night's sleep. Felt great. Mm-hmm. Yeah, thanks. Listen, I know it's way too late, really, and I feel so foolish. Do you think we might un-cancel the party? Mm-hmm. Yeah, right. Really? Great! I think that'd be great. I can call ... what's that? You'll call the others? Oh, thanks, that would be amazing. No, I can make the dinner. Yeah, ham, I'm thinking. I don't know, do you want to make your scalloped potatoes?"

She went on like that for a couple more minutes. We saw the daemon dance in and try to whisper something to her at one point, but she didn't seem to pay him the slightest bit of attention. Finally, he turned to look in our direction, glowered, and danced away.

I looked at Gentleness as Heaven was concluding her call. My new grandmotherly friend smiled at me, and nodded, and winked. I held my hand up to give her a "high five," and luckily remembered before our hands met to make it a *very gentle* clap.

We peeked back to see Heaven put her trophy in a more prominent spot on the counter; then, a moment later, she walked toward the living room. We could hear her opening a plastic bin, and a couple of boxes. A minute later, she came back to the kitchen with something in her hand. It was a little figurine of a Christmas caroler, from which she removed the top hat and placed it over the cap on the head of the crouching batter that adorned the top of the trophy. She stepped back to admire her work. And she giggled.

When Heaven left the kitchen to head that way, we two elves crept to the living room and snuck behind the couch to observe. Over the next few minutes, we watched Heaven McCready unpack her XMAS boxes and bins, and to start decorating her home. From a long box she removed sections of an artificial evergreen tree, which she put together on its stand in front of the picture window. She placed runners on tables, candles in holders, and garland draped over curtain rods. She placed one ornament on the tree, then stopped to retrieve a small stack of compact discs from one of the bins. She inserted one of the discs, and as she placed the other ornaments on her tree, she hummed and sang along with the festive music coming from her stereo speakers.

Sleigh Ride by the Boston Pops started to play. She stopped, and let out a hearty laugh. "Perry Miller! Tommy Como!" she said aloud, and quietly laughed again.

When *The Christmas Waltz* began to play, Heaven stopped what she was doing and began digging around in another bin. She came up with a sprig of artificial mistletoe. She picked up a stepping stool and made her way toward the front entry.

The daemon danced along behind her, continually trying to whisper in Heaven's ear.

"I know you're here," she said aloud, as she attached the mistletoe to the light fixture just inside the front door. "You're always here, hanging around, aren't you? I know you'll never leave me alone. Just can't get enough of me."

I had a brief bout of anxiety upon hearing Heaven say that. It quickly went away, though, replaced by sudden glee when she said "I didn't get all I wanted of you, either, funny boy."

The daemon stomped out of the room. He seemed to realize that Heaven hadn't chosen him, after all. He had just witnessed his utter defeat. His Target had gladness. She'd rediscovered *her Joy!* And her sorrows and sighings were fleeing away, stomping out of her like the daemon stomped out of her living room. Because Heaven McCready was now talking to her dear, late, beloved, funny-boy husband. She was now spending time in her memory with the Martin she married—not the one she buried.

Gentleness put her arm around me, and nodded toward the back door. As we crept silently out into the crisp Denver December morning, Heaven

McCready was singing along to that Perry Miller Tommy Como classic, *Joy to the World*.

"And Heaven and nature sing! And Heaven and nature sing! And Hea-VEN, and Heaven, and nature sing!"

* * *

The door to the executive conference room opened, and Meekness poked his head out. "We're ready for ya, babe," he said. I left the waiting room, where I'd practically paced a ditch into the oakwood floor, and slowly trudged through the door.

The Saint was seated at the far head of the table, and The Nine at chairs around each side. Meekness took his seat toward the near end, and I slowly seated myself in the empty chair next to him, at the end opposite Nick.

"You should stand, kiddo," Meekness whispered. "It's a better look."

I stood.

Frank, the Joy Elf, spoke up from his seat at The Saint's right. "Heaven McCready has found her Joy," he said. "Let's show our appreciation for her, a true elect daughter of The Lord!"

Everyone began solemnly applauding by rapping the table with their knuckles. There were smiles and nods all around.

"Now, Lim'rick, it's time for you to explain to us all what, if anything, *you* have found."

I took off my cap, and removed from it the crumpled parchment on which I'd made my notes. I uncrumpled it, making noise that I'm sure was dreadfully out of place in the otherwise silent room. After what seemed like forever, I cleared my throat and began to read.

> A recent reveal... review of this year's most popular gift requests from Nice Listees revealed that video games and consoles, video game accessories, other games, movies, movie tickets, concert tickets and other amusements again top the list, continuing a trend of many years, from everyone from pre-teens to unemployed forty-year-olds. This, um, trend, indicates that, unlike in ages past, that, that there is a sort of trend. This trend, if we examine, um, if we ...

"Lim'rick," The Saint interrupted, "you can write that up and send it to us via inter-elfin mail. Right now, we'd just like to hear what you've learned. Just talk to us."

I recrumpled my notes and tossed them into my unused chair. I re-cleared my throat, and stared at my stylish elf-slippers.

"You've got this," I heard Faith whisper.

"Just take a deep breath, and relax," Peace added.

I finally found my voice.

"Okay, thank you Sir, and Sirs. And, um, Madames, I guess." I looked at Gentleness, who gave me a reassuring wink and nod.

"What I learned is that our world is in deep snow right now, and certainly in need of Joy. Just look at these figures," I said, picking up my wadded parchment, waving it around, and tossing it onto the polished tabletop. "A whole generation, and maybe the next one, spending all their time and money and God-given energy on nothing but keeping themselves constantly entertained, and, well, distracted, I guess. Distracted from what, though? I don't know. All I know is that it doesn't seem to be working all that well for them. All this entertainment, and yet we have all these people who seem constantly unhappy, and depressed, and even angry around the edges. Why in the world—"

"You're ranting," Frank said. "Get to the point. If you have one."

"Right," I said. "Sorry, Sir."

"What did *you* learn?"

"I learned a lot, Sir, about Joy. Real Joy. It's a gift from God. It isn't happiness, or fun, or whatever. In fact, everybody gets unhappy from time to time, but if we have true Joy ... and Love ... and Goodness ... and, well, *all* of us ... running always in our soul, the daemons that target us can't win. Without Joy, life's imperfections are catastrophes. Every skinned knee is a devastation. Joy can share the room even with unhappiness, and eventually, it banishes those feelings of sadness. Joy laughs at unhappiness! But without Joy, you lose the ability to laugh the good laugh. At life's little bumps, at the most unpleasant circumstances ... even at yourself! Without Joy, you're at the mercy of your daemons, who constantly whisper poisonous thoughts of shame, and dread, and fear, and even utter despair."

I took a breath. Frank and The Saint looked at each other. Some of my new friends smiled.

"Is that it?" Frank asked.

"I guess so," I said. "I'd only add that I've learned that *fun* comes from games, and entertainment comes from shows and stuff. Jokes come from wit. But Joy—*true Joy*—comes from the Lord, and *only* from Him. And here on Earth, I've come to believe that Joy is experienced as nothing more than the leftover aroma, so to speak, of God's entertainment of Himself . . . of a clever joke the Father tells the Son inside us . . . of the holy amusement at the comedy we play out, every day of our physical existence. And even the faintest scent of holy happiness lingering in your soul is enough to fill you to overflowing with real, pure Joy."

I took a deep breath.

"Are you finished?" Frank asked.

"Yes, Sir, I'm finished."

"Well, Lim'rick . . ."

"I think when you finally go home to Him, that's when the Lord gives you the punchline," I added. "That's when you finally, truly *get it*. And that's why I believe that the heavenly kingdom must be filled with happy music, and with the sound of millions *laughing* out of pure, undiluted love for The Father. Laughing the laughter of *pure Joy*."

Nobody spoke. Nobody moved. When I realized they were all waiting to see whether more words would tumble out of me, I sat down, partly because I still hadn't slept much and needed the rest ... and partly to keep from saying anything else.

* * *

One thing you should know about elves is that we're very humble, especially The Nine. So I won't tell you about all the thunderous applause, and hugging, and backslapping that ended up happening. And I won't tell you about Frank's retirement ceremony later that day, or about the part of the celebration when I took the top-secret oath and got my induction as the brand-new Joy Elf. All I'll say is that Frank's full name was engraved on his retirement plaque, and that's how I found out it was Frankincense.

About the Author

Michael Hume is the international bestselling author of *The Innkeeper of Bethlehem* and *The 95th Christmas*, and the award winning singer/songwriter behind the acclaimed holiday album, *The Christmas In Me*.

In the summer of 2024, Michael walked 272 miles from his home in southern Colorado to the Monastery of Christ in the Desert (Abiquiu, New Mexico), where he continued in retreat. . . . he called this his 2024 "Quest," and considers the seven weeks to be a significant blessing in his life.

"I got to spend several hours a day, walking alone with The Lord, through this amazing flower garden He created," Michael says. "I could not have done it without divine help, and I also have my wife to thank for her incredible and generous support."

Michael brought home from his Quest a generous renewal of Joy, Peace, Humility, and much Gratitude.

And, of course, *Mrs. McCready and The Joy Elf.*

Michael lives with his "heavenly" wife, Kathryn, and their faithful canine companion, Poppins.